To Wayne & Frances Toussaint
—J.R.

Text copyright © 2004 by Jen Hochhauser
Illustrations copyright © 2004 by Teetersaw, Inc.
All rights reserved
CIP Data is available.
Published in the United States 2004 by
Blue Apple Books
515 Valley Street, Maplewood, N.J. 07040
www.blueapplebooks.com
Distributed in the U.S. by Chronicle Books

First Edition
Printed in China
ISBN: 1-59354-061-2
1 3 5 7 9 10 8 6 4 2

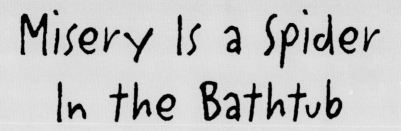

Misery Is a Spider In the Bathtub

Jen Hochhauser

drawings by Jennifer Rapp

🍎 blue Apple Books

Some days are terrific.
You win every game.
There's an "A" on your paper,
A star by your name.

Sometimes it feels
like nothing goes right.
You stay in bed
And keep out of sight.

You feel like a piece
Of yesterday's toast.
Of everyone hated,
You're hated the most.

Instead of singing
A misery song,
Read on to find out
What else can go wrong!

Misery is when your
splinter won't come out
and your mom has to
tweeze and squeeze it.

Misery is when your dad says:
"If you're too full to eat spinach,
then you must be too full for
apple pie with ice cream."

Misery is when you have to wear a hat
after you requested "just a little trim."

Misery is taking a bite of too-hot pizza
when the cheese is still bubbly
and trying to juggle it with your tongue
while you reach for a sip
of cold water.

Misery is when your brother shows you his chewed food.

Misery is finding out
your mom is pregnant.

Misery is when
the nurse rubs on the alcohol
and you have to be still
and listen to her say:
"This will only sting for a minute."

Misery is not being able to call your parents to come and take you home from a sleep-over.

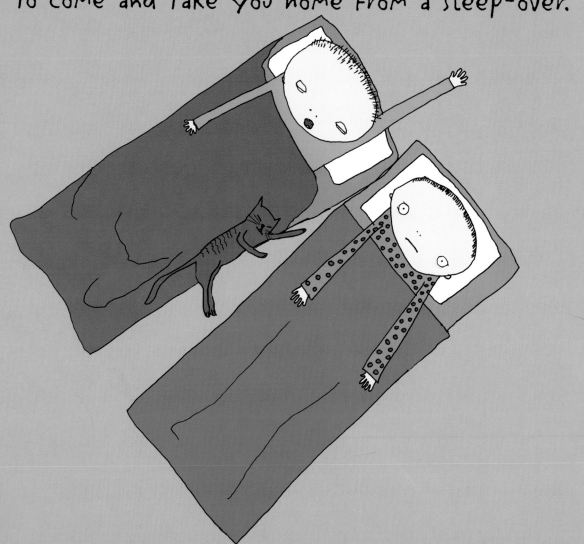

Misery is when your mom decides that nail biting is a bad habit which should be stopped immediately.

Misery is when
you've swallowed too much,
too-cold ice cream,
too fast.

Misery is being too grown-up to be baby-sat for and too young to baby-sit.

Misery is writing to thank
Aunt Kate for the "beautiful" birthday
present, which you know she expects you
to wear the next time she visits.

Misery is listening to Ethan's brother practice the clarinet.

Misery is explaining
to the doctor how
the jellybean became
stuck in your nose.

Misery is listening to your mother shout:
"Did you remember to go to the bathroom?"
as you leave for a walk around the block.

Misery is having a curfew.

Some days have miseries
In all kinds of ways.
Hope your tomorrow's
Not one of these days.

Hope in the morning
Not a thing will go wrong.
And you won't be singing
A misery song.